This book belongs to:

_____

_____

_____

To Lili, my greatest source of inspiration...
To Tao and Maé. To Sandrine, a thousand thank-yous.

Little Unicorn is ANGRY

Aurélie Chien Chow Chine

LITTLE, BROWN AND COMPANY

NEW YORK   BOSTON

This is Little Unicorn.
He is very much like all the other little unicorns....

Sometimes, **Little Unicorn** is happy.
Sometimes, he is **not** happy.
Sometimes, he is sad.
Sometimes, he is scared.
Sometimes, he is angry.

These are emotions.

And **Little Unicorn** feels all kinds of emotions.
Just like you.

But there is something that makes **Little Unicorn** special:
He has a **magical mane**!

When all is well, his mane shines
with the colors of the rainbow.

But when all isn't well, his mane changes...
and its color shows just what he feels.

Happy

Jealous

Angry

Guilty

Shy

Scared

Stubborn

Sad

How does **Little Unicorn** feel today?

Awful!

His heart feels dark and stormy,
and he's going to tell us why.

And you, how do you feel today?

Great

Good

Fine

Not good

Bad

Awful

Now, why does **Little Unicorn** feel
so terrible today?

Most of the time, he doesn't have a care in
the world, like there's not a cloud in the sky.

At home and at school, Little Unicorn feels fine.

But there are some days when
nothing seems to go his way.

And that upsets **Little Unicorn**.

On days when he decides to go play in
the garden and it suddenly starts raining,
Little Unicorn is annoyed.

When he has to go to school
but he doesn't want to walk there,
Little Unicorn is upset.

And if Papa refuses to carry him,
Little Unicorn is angry.

When Mama calls him for bath time
but he doesn't want to take a bath,
Little Unicorn is upset.

And when it's time to get out of
the water but he still wants to play,
Little Unicorn is angry.

When he decides to do something all by himself,
just like a big unicorn, but he can't do it,
Little Unicorn is upset.

Sometimes he even rolls around on the floor
and kicks his feet! That's when
he feels very angry!

So very angry!

It feels like he has a giant stormy cloud in his head.
A cloud filled with lightning.

What if, instead of waiting for the cloud to go away,
he could chase it away?

He can! He uses his breath.

When you feel a cloud of anger inside,
you can do this **breathing exercise** to blow it away, too.

Breathing exercise
to blow away
the anger cloud

1. **Little Unicorn** closes his eyes.
He imagines the giant cloud in his head.
He breathes in through his nose,
inflating his belly, as he stretches his arms
down his body and closes his fists.

2 **Little Unicorn** holds his breath.
He shrugs his shoulders quickly a few times, up and down,
up and down, as if he's pumping all his anger into the cloud.

3 **Little Unicorn** relaxes his shoulders and hands,
and he blows all the air out hard.
He pretends to blow away his giant anger cloud!

Little Unicorn does this exercise **three times.**

It takes at least **three breaths**
to blow away the very last of the lightning!

At last, he begins to breathe normally.
Now that he's chased away the clouds from his head,
the **beautiful sun** can shine in.

Ah, **Little Unicorn** feels much calmer.
His good mood is back, and
the rainbow has returned to his mane.

The next time things don't go his way,
it'll be okay. He'll keep his cool.

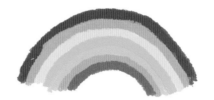

If you use your breathing
to replace a storm with the sun,
you might feel calmer, too.
And your **smile** will return!

Don't miss these other stories about
Little Unicorn!

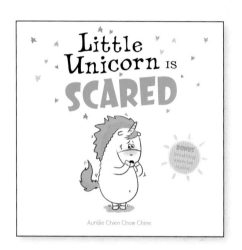

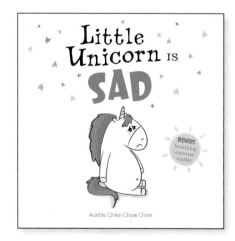

Coming soon!

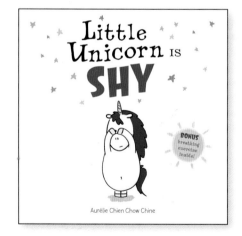

Coming soon!